CODY GRAVES PRESENTS

HORROR WEEKLY

HORROR WEEKLY

By

The Butchered Writers

2 Dark Harvest

A VERY SPECIAL THANK YOU TO SARAH BAUER FOR JOINING US AS THE NEW EDITOR OF HORROR WEEKLY

A VERY SPECIAL THANK YOU TO OUR AMAZINGLY TALENTED ART DESIGNER BROOKE LOCKMAN

A VERY SPECIAL THANK YOU TO ADINA TROUTMAN FOR CREATING OUR BOOK COVER

ALL STORIES

REVISED

BY

CODY GRAVES

Continue At Your Own Risk

Horror Weekly

The Butchered Writers is a group of independent authors who have joined together to bring you the most terrifying stories that will stay with you long after you turn the page

CONTENTS

TAINTED MEAT

BY

BROOKE LOCKMAN

It's the morning of Thanksgiving day, and my stomach is already turning from the smell of the cooked turkey making its way throughout the house.

I'm vegetarian so, I can't stand the smell or even the thought of it without it making me want to release a steaming pile of bile everywhere.

It's bad enough I have to watch my family stuff their greasy mouths every year with what was once a majestic living creature.

Looking out of my bedroom window, I see my neighbor is out there and he is patting my dad on the back for his successful hunt, and in my eyes for murdering that innocent turkey.

"Rebecca! Come on down and help me set the table please" yelled my mother.

She ain't much better I thought as I descended the steps. She might not take part in the killing of the poor animal but she still eats it and that's enough for me to resent her.

Letting out an annoyed huff of air, I went to the silverware drawer and grabbed enough utensils for the whole family that should arrive any minute now.

By the time I'm done setting the table my aunt and uncle come storming in with obnoxiously loud laughter and treys of green bean casserole and pumpkin pie.

I decided to go back up to my room until it was time to eat. I can't stand any of them, all they care about is bringing home an eight-pointer buck and politics. This day is already horrible enough how can someone be thankful for taking the life of a breathing creature? The fact that I'm forced to watch them devour it every year makes me sick, but not next year, next year I'll be at college and I won't have to witness their inhumane acts.

"Everyone! Turkey is done!" I heard my dad proudly announce throughout the house.

"And the torture begins," I say under my breath with a knot growing deep within my stomach. As I enter the dining room everyone's eyes turn to meet me.

"Ah, Rebecca! Are you going to try the turkey this year? I heard you're father tried some new seasonings, it's supposed to make it extra juicy!" said my Uncle Joey with a sarcastic smirk on his face knowing damn well what my answer would be.

I chose to ignore him and give an eye roll in response as I made my way to my seat at the end of the long rectangular table. My family starts with a prayer, I look around at everyone with judgment.

I stack my plate with sweet potatoes, corn on the cob, and green bean casserole knowing that's as good as it's getting for me tonight. Honestly, I don't know if I'll even be able to keep it down.

Everyone begins to dig in, I keep my head held low, hearing them rip the fried carcass apart and argue about which parts are the best and juiciest... This is Hell.

I flicked the vegetables around on my plate with my fork trying to keep my mind occupied. After hearing them smack and slurp down chunks of greasy meat my appetite was replaced with a trail of hot acid working its way up my gullet.

I was about to ask to be excused when I felt a vibrating sensation coming from my pocket followed by an alarm coming from every direction. The whole family brought out their phones to see what the emergency was about.

WARNING

"Warning, deadly parasitic worms found in wild turkey, for further information, click the link below," my uncle announced with an uneasy tone in his voice as he slowly spat out his half-chewed bite.

All of our eyes met the skeletal remains of the turkey on the counter. There was nothing left but bones and chunks of fat. My family became deathly quiet as they all shared terrified looks.

"W-w-what do we do now?" My aunt nervously asked while frantically looking to everyone for an answer.

"Maybe we are safe. Maybe we got a clean one, no need to panic, right?" my dad said as he picked around and examined the carcass for any visible evidence.

I found this horrific distraction the perfect time to make my escape back to my room. As I stood up and slowly backed toward the stairs I could hear my aunt mumbling with my uncle who attempted to calm her while they reviewed the warning message.

I went to the bathroom to wash up. I felt bad enough at dinner, but the worms were the final nail in the coffin for me.

As I splashed water on my face in the sink I think about how fucked up karma can be, but also how fair it can be.

As I blindly reach for the hand towel to wipe my face dry I hear screaming from downstairs.

Rushing down the stairs I stop dead in my tracks when I reach the bottom step. My uncle's hunched over in pain, my mom at his side rubbing his back and whispering "It's okay Joey just breathe"

My aunt is freaking out ten times worse as the pain hits her next. My dad stands beside her motionless, horrified at the sight before his eyes when he is suddenly struck, dropping to the floor he moans in agony.

Joey makes a wrenching gag as his hands move from his stomach to his throat, his veins budging out of his neck and his face so hard. I think they could burst with any more pressure.

Projectile vomit explodes from his mouth. Chunks of gore splash all over the leftover stuffing. Uncle Joey collapsed to the ground, his body profusely shook as I saw crimson-colored slugs mixed with foam start erupting out of his nose and mouth at a rapid speed.

My mother jumped back from the shock with her hand over her mouth as she witnessed her brother turn into a grisly horror show.

I stood there with my mouth agape as I watched piles of squirming carnage spew from my uncle's openings.

My aunt screamed until her voice was replaced by a splashing gargle.

My attention darted in her direction in time to see her jaw drop, completely dislocating. Bloody drool flowed over her bottom row of teeth like a crimson waterfall.

I looked closer and saw something working its way out of her.

Inch By Inch

I watched her jaw completely detached and dangle by loose stands of flesh that tore from the seams as an enormous white worm crawled out of her mutilated face.

It had rows of needle-like teeth protruding out like a tongue frantically searching for something to latch onto. As it slithered the rest of its way out.

I ran in fear of becoming the worm's next meal, I hurried to my room to call for help. I slammed and locked the door behind me.

I get my cell and see the battery has died. Not wasting any time I rush for my charger and then move to the far corner to plug it in. I beg for the screen to come to life.

OH MY GOD!!

I hear my mother's blood-curdling scream from below.
I covered my ears in complete terror as I swayed side to side, praying to God that this wasn't happening.

My phone lit up. I took a deep breath and shakingly dialed 911

My heart was racing, I heard the sloshing sounds getting closer to me.

CLOSER BY THE SECOND

"911, what's your emergency?"

Before I could open my mouth, I began to see slimy gore-smothered worms forcing their bloated bodies under my doorway.

I Move closer to frantically stomp on any piece of them I can hit. The pressure against my door quickly increased and I could see the hinges given away to the force on the other side.

The hinges give out and my door assaults me, knocking me to the carpet and my phone under the bed. I crawl away. Looking back I see the giant white worm that feasted upon my aunt's intestines. It flops on top of me, knocking my breath loose from my lungs. I feel a pain quickly shoot throughout my entire body.

The worm worked its way to my chest with its elongated mouth spinning like a drill bit making chunks out of my flesh.

I took a deep breath of copper when I opened my mouth to release the agony. I knew I was about to be finished with the other creatures closing in.

I hit the worm and rolled to my side, its body smashing its smaller companions. I got to my feet and ran for the window. They were right behind me. I put my hands on the sill, it doesn't lift. I panic to unlock the latches. They are at my feet. I slide the panel open, the white worm jumps for me.

"Hello? Ma'am, are you there? What's your emergency?" The operator asked.

"HELLO?"

"MA'AM?"

A Bean Family Thanksgiving

By

Jimi Peranteau

"Why are you doing this?" Michelle
cried out.

"Why shouldn't I? Tradition is
strong in this family girl." Mark kneels
to speak in a more face-to-face setting
with his captive. "I could ask the same of
you. Of all of you! Every year it's the
same thing. Halloween comes around
and a group of you decide it's *okay* to
desecrate the resting place of our family.
And every year! it's always the same

outcome. Four of you go missing, and our Thanksgiving is complete."

Mark rises to his feet as a cellar door creaks open. Heavy footsteps echo throughout the cellar as three of his family members make their way to the prisoners. Jeff, a large disfigured man enters first. His presence demands their full attention. As he steps into view, Michelle's face turns to a cold, pale shade. The chains that bind her rattle as she trembles in fear.

"Hmmm," Jeff says while looking around the dimly lit room. His eyes glanced at each of the victims. First is Sharon, a slim blonde-haired girl. "I know your type," he says. "You're the one who catches the attention of every teenage misfit who shows up to the high school football games. But you know this already don't you? Sluts like you know the only reason those imbeciles even bother to live is to stare at cheerleader whores. You ain't no better girl."

He makes his way to the next captive. This one is Johnny. A muscle-bound snob that flaunts his parent's fortune as if it were his own. "This one, the prick," he continues, "I doubt he will be of any use." His words are cold, and blank as he drags a small hatchet across Johnny's jawline. "Assholes always leave a shitty aftertaste." His attention turns to Molly, the brunette bookworm of the group.

"Well now, don't you look tasteful." He comes to a stop just inches in front of the terrified brunette. "Let me guess, you found yourself with these dimwits out of sheer desperation to make a few new friends. To make at least one decent memory of high school. Pity, you chose wrong." Jeff grunts as he grabs a fistful of her hair, pulling her to her feet. She feels the cold makeshift wall press against her back. Chains rattle and smack against the stone wall as she tries to find her balance. Jeff's rigid skin scrapes against hers as he inhales deeply through his nose. His nostrils flare as he catches the scent from her neck. A slight moan of approval races over her ears as he runs his tongue from the base of her neck to the top of her temple. "Mmm," he says, "just the right amount of salt!" As he pushes himself away from Molly, a grunt of disapproval is all he offers to Michelle. Jeff never really was a fan of redheads.

An older man makes his way into the cellar. He brings not only a young boy with him but a large cart with a twenty-two-pound turkey placed on top. "Are you finished yet?" The old man asks the playful brothers.

"Three weeks they've been here boys. Three weeks, and you pick today to play with your food. Have we not taught you better?" The old man places his hand gently on young Patrick's shoulder, guiding him over so he can begin the lesson. "Listen here boy, every family has its traditions for the holidays. Each has its own recipes, and its own way of cooking. Today I will teach you our family's way of preparing the Thanksgiving feast. You pay attention, this is important, this is our way of life."

Patrick, eager to learn, gives his father his full attention. "First we need to prepare the meat before we can cook it." He grabs a handful of peppercorns and a large meat injector. "We need to first poke some holes throughout the body." As he begins to demonstrate for Patrick, Mark begins his assault on Johnny. Together, the father and son penetrate the bodies. As Johnny becomes a pin cushion for the family's box of sewing needles, the turkey receives its own puncture wounds. "With each hole we make, we place a single peppercorn at the bottom of it." The old father pushes the injector into the breast of the turkey once more while the young girls are forced to watch as Mark inserts another needle into the chest cavity of his play toy. The needle pushes its way past skin, and fat layers, burying itself just beside a beating heart.

"Adrenaline is key, Patrick," the father explains, while pointing towards the group of captives. "It's produced and introduced into the bloodstream during stressful situations. It can keep a body going when needed giving us the boost that we desire to come out on top. Do you know what else adrenaline will do?"

Young Patrick shakes his head, answering his father with a subtle no. "Adrenaline creates a special flavor for the blood. It's a special chemical my boy, and it makes the human blood taste much different." Mark begins to deliver several brutal strikes to Johnny's torso while his brother Jeff forces the girls to watch. " Increased adrenaline is introduced into the bloodstream, the more stressed and scared they are. That is why they watch. They know they will die down here, so their heart races. The more we show them, the better the reward. That reward is an ingredient that only the human body can create." He turns to his sons and calls for them to listen. "It's time... End them."

Jeff smiles as he spins the hatchet in his hand. "It's Thanksgiving girls! Tell me, what are you thankful for? Wait, second thought, let me figure it out! Each of you are pretty damn thankful you're not this guy! Am I right?" Jeff laughs as he grabs Johnny's hair, tilting his head backward. His hatchet now falls at full force, burying itself into Johnny's face. His nose splits in two as the blade burrows deeper. The sound of skull cracking fills the air. The blunt blade separates the hemispheres of the brain from one another. Jeff pulls the hatchet out, and swings again, and again. Bits of bone and brain matter fling from Johnny's face and stick to the floor. His body jolts as the last sparks of bodily function cease to exist. "Do you see the look on their face boy? That is how you know the blood is ready. One final task left. We must collect the blood now."

Mark grabs Sharon, and after unlocking her bindings he drags her over to his father. The old man places a small metal tub on the floor. Mark leans her forward. She screams and kicks, desperation and the will to survive taking over her body.

"There it is boy, that is the adrenaline we are looking for. This is the

moment we collect our prize." The old
father explains as Mark slices Sharon's
neck open with a large fillet knife. Her
blood pulses out, spilling into the tub.
One by one they kick and scream, yet
their blood is drained.

"While your brothers gather the
blood for us, we need to season the
turkey. Gently cut the skin free of the
breast meat. We need to peel it back to
expose the flesh. Then take a quarter cup
of oregano, and mix it with a quarter cup
of thyme, and a tablespoon of rubbed
sage. Rub the mixture onto the meat,
really rub it in. You need it covered.
Then place the skin back, pressing it
onto the meat as best as you can." Patrick
watches, taking in each step his father
teaches him. "Next, we marinate the
bird. Which is what your brothers have

been doing. It takes three gallons of blood to cover the bird in its entirety. It must be exact. No more. No less." He places the turkey into a large pot, every inch of it becoming submerged. "We leave it to marinate overnight, tomorrow we smoke it."

After a night of marinating, Patrick brings the turkey to his father, who waits outside in the backyard. As he reaches him, he notices only one full body remains, Molly the brunette. Placed adjacent to Molly's lower abdomen Sharon. Sharon's abdominal skin had been sliced open, and hollowed out, leaving plenty of room. "Put that turkey in here," the old man points to the partial torso. Once inside, he stitches Sharon closed. The father and son lift what is left of Sharon and place her into the empty torso of Molly. After a final stitching, Patrick helps his father place the body into the smoker. "And now we wait."

Several hours pass before their feast is finally ready. The sun has begun to set as an old woman yells throughout the home. As the family gathers around the dinner table, Patrick and his father wheel in the main course for the Bean family Thanksgiving. They lift up their hard work and place it onto the center of the table. The covering is removed, revealing their main course.

Molly lays on the table, her birthing canal completely removed and filled with Stove Top Stuffing. Patrick cuts open her torso, the skin racing in opposite directions. Inside Molly's torso and hidden within Sharon's lower abdomen sits a blood-red turkey. Her breasts have been detached and replaced with side dishes. Her head resting in an upward position. The skull cap and brain were removed and filled with biscuits and rolls.

Before the family can enjoy the feast, their mother makes everyone at the table say something they are thankful for. One by one they rattle off nonsense and memories until finally the old woman instructs them to take a seat. Just before the first forkful is taken, the old woman simply says...

BON APPETIT!

MEET THE CARVER

BY

CODY GRAVES

My name is Leah, and I want to tell you about the worst day of my life.

Last thanksgiving...

The day that took the ones I love and left this blackness inside me. The day I lost my humanity and became this cold shell with nothing and no one left. Except for him.

My parents were loving caring people with hearts too big to ignore someone's pain. That was why my mom canceled our normal Thanksgiving plans which consisted of a yearly big family get-together. Instead, we would travel out of town to be with Aunt Priscilla.

There was a dark cloud hanging over the past few weeks due to my Uncle passing away recently from an illness. I didn't know him well, he was nothing more than some brief childhood memories. So as sad as it is to say, his death didn't have much impact on me.

Mom and her sister hadn't been very close throughout the years. But she dropped everything to be there for her. That was the kind of person she was.

The drive was long but nothing too extreme. We got to the large house that sat on a private piece of land, it felt like its own little world. The front gate was rusty, reminding me of a Gothic cemetery. The yard was unkempt and neglected.

The house wasn't much better. Tall hedges stood before the entrance. Worn steps led to a wide covered porch. The paint of the pillars had chipped off long ago and some of the shudders were hanging on by a nail.

We walked the cracked sidewalk to the door. My mom knocked and let herself in. The place gave me the creeps. It was basically maintained by the Firefly family.

We went into the dusty clutter-filled home. Somehow the inside was worse than the outside. I know I shouldn't judge. Her husband of thirty-plus years just passed. but it is clear they lived like this for what could look like more than a century.

Priscilla sat in a chair by a TV that was older than me.
She was glued to the blaring news, barely acknowledging our presence. Looking back, I should have recognized that moment as a sign from a higher power. A message we were too blind to see.

REPORTER:

Police are still searching for the man responsible for a long line of gruesome murders. Officers encountered the culprit late last night, he is now known as the Thanksgiving Carver. Officer Sarandon, stated he got a round off in the killer's leg but lost him in the pursuit. The Thanksgiving Carver has not yet been identified but has left seventeen dead in the wake of his chaos.

He is armed and considered extremely dangerous

Mom took the remote and lowered the volume to steal my aunt's attention. Aunt Priscilla got up and tightly hugged each of us, then moped her way from the living room to the kitchen.

Dad brought in the food Mom prepared and packed for us. At the time, my biggest concern was eating too much and going back to school looking like a bloated whale. I wish I knew the danger we were in. Outside the house lurking, was someone who had no remorse. Someone with no comprehension of the word mercy. Now, I question if he was in the yard, or maybe on the porch trying to peer through the windows. The endless possibilities drive me mad when

I reflect, and it is the only thing I still think about. I wonder what was going through his mind at that point. Did he have a plan? It will always be a mystery.

After turkey, mashed potatoes, stuffing, and cranberry sauce, we found ourselves sitting in silence.

"I miss him so much," Aunt Priscilla said with her fork grazing her pumpkin pie dessert. Mom moved to her side to comfort her.

"C'mon, kiddo. Let's give them some time," Dad said, nudging me to follow him to the living room.

They talked for a while. Around eight o'clock, Dad decided it was time to load the car and go. He quietly gathered the food containers. I joined him wanting to take a break from sitting on the couch.

I followed Dad to the SUV through the tall grass. He opened the hatch and set everything in.

"Almost time to hit the road, kid". He said, wrapping his arm around me as we traveled back to the door.

When we were walking past my aunt's hedges, I heard a sudden commotion from the unknown. The impact was instant, I closed my eyes hearing a grunting yell as I dropped to the ground with my dad falling on top of me. My leg felt like it snapped from his weight, crushing my body into the grass.

Dad quickly returned to his feet. I stayed down grasping my leg with tears forcing through my closed eyes.

I heard a struggle while everything was dark behind my eyelids. When I opened them, I saw my dad engaged in a deadly fight for survival with a stranger.

A man with long messy hair in a trench coat over a suit clawed my dad's face. He had bulging psychotic eyes. Dad wasn't weak but he was overtaken by the sneak attack.

They continued to battle. Grasping my injured knee, I limped to the porch to get help.

When I turned back, I saw Dad facing me with the man behind him. He was choking the life and light out of his eyes.

The attacker released him, allowing him to drop into the tall grass. Then he reached into his coat and brought out a long jagged knife.

"NO!"

I screamed as the steel blade dug into his flesh, claiming his breath in the blink of an eye. Taking him from me, forever.

My mother opened the door to come out and check on the noise. Her face twisted in horror, her body almost falling out from under her at the heinous sight.

I pushed her inside as the deranged killer brought his glare over to us. We slammed and locked the door. I could barely stand but found the strength to drag Mom to the kitchen where Aunt Priscilla was still seated.

We heard the window shatter behind us. Mom was in shock, she couldn't handle the reality of what she had witnessed. Aunt Priscilla took us to the back door.

There was clutter everywhere. She desperately started throwing her belongings to the side. An old vacuum, lamp, and boxes of forgotten magazines.

The man made his way into her home. When I turned back I saw him limping his way through the living room toward us. His leg was injured, forcing him to stagger. I realized he was the one the police were after. My stomach turned in disbelief. He's The Carver, and he was there to spill all of our blood.

I screamed trying to help my aunt, bawling in the process as he hobbled closer.

My mother screamed,

"Stay away from my baby!"

She left our side and put herself
between her family and the
monstrous human a few feet away.

The Carver grabbed her and
forced her body over to the stove.
He lived up to his name as he cut
deep into her throat with a vicious
strike.

I was frozen. She was so close, but I
couldn't do anything to save her. My
aunt got the back door open and forced
me out into the enclosed porch. I fell on
top of a pile of garbage bags.
She grabbed a candlestick and
charged the murderer, hitting him in the
head. He stumbled away for an instant

before he turned back around and stabbed his knife through my aunt's defensive hand.

She screamed in agony. He ripped the blade out and then pulled her closer to sink his teeth into her face. Feasting on a piece of her.

I stared off in a daze through the house, my vision blurred, I was paralyzed by fear. He whipped his head my way. I saw his rabid eyes with the torn bloody flesh in his mouth like some sort of wild animal.

I hurried to the door that leads out onto the deck planning for an escape, but there was too much clutter blocking it from opening. I fought to stand on the bags beneath me. The useless junk and storage would be the death of me. He jammed his knife into my aunt's stomach and with a twist of the handle she was finished.

HE CAME FOR ME NEXT

I grabbed an old toaster from the pile of junk and used it to break a small glass window adjacent to the door.

The Carver started his journey over the bags. I jumped up to crawl out. The broken glass cut into my stomach and scraped my body as I slithered my way to freedom.

I FELT HIM GRAB ME

His hand clutched around my ankle. I felt the tip of his knife slice along my leg. The pain from my injuries was excruciating, but I refused to go down without a fight. I kicked my legs with everything I had. Panicking, I fought, yanking from his hold. I managed to kick him in the face and break free.

I fell out of the window onto the outer deck. My heart felt like it couldn't take much more as it pounded out of my chest. The Carver fought his way through the door as I crawled away. I saw my aunt's grill in the corner as an opportunity.

The Carver made his way outside and limped his way closer to me. Both of our right legs were injured.

HIS KNIFE WAS SOAKED WITH THE BLOOD OF MY LOVED ONES

He licked his lips as he approached.

HE KNEELED TO GRAB ME

I shifted my body and fired my shot. Digging a BBQ fork deep into his ribs, I watched the horror on his face come to life. He screamed, his mouth was so close that I could feel his warm breath on my skin. The sound of his crying pain was like sweet music.

He fell back on the deck with the fork still jammed deep into him. He dropped his knife from my unexpected attack. He rolled over and began to crawl to the stairs. I grabbed his weapon and jumped to bury it deep into his back, carving The Carver.

Before I could finish him, I caught his elbow to my face, knocking me hard to the ground. His knife came with me as I dropped to the deck.

I watched him tumble down the stairs and run out of sight into the woods. It took me a long time to find the strength to get up. I didn't go after him. I returned to my Mother's side, but she was long gone. Everyone was gone.

The hospital was able to fix my wounds but unfortunately, there wasn't a remedy for all the damage the Carver had caused me. I didn't give the police his knife. I kept it for a special day.

It's been two years now.

It's Thanksgiving again.

THIS TIME I'M OUTSIDE HIS HOUSE

Samuel Bibbit. It's time to pay for your sins. Enjoy your dinner. Because soon you will face the monster you created.

YOU WILL BE CARVED...

FEED THE POOR

By

James Fisher

"The movers always beat me here," Kurt Thomlin mumbled to himself through chapped lips. Overhead, the heavens had darkened, the sun's last rays of warmth and hope extinguishing with the onset of an undoubtedly cruel winter.

The dumpster which he had been attempting to scour for good boxes was another dead end. It seemed everyone was skipping town or moving lately, and it had left him in quite a bind.

Kurt's box shelter needed reinforcing, and this was his only way to source them. He put his gnarled fingers on his gaunt face, stroking an unruly gray beard as his steely blue eyes surveyed the horizon. That day, he had already gone through twelve dumpsters on the commercial side of town and only had one decent box to show for it. The sudden drought of resources had him in a panic, especially with a harsh season ahead and no other means of sourcing boxes.

"There's always the—*rich*—side of town," Kurt mumbled to himself, his patchy silver hair falling over his eyes. He swept it back, putting his old Boston Bruins cap back on, and leaving the alleyway. Something had to happen and fast. The following weekend was showing to be in the record lows. Boston got cold enough—he didn't want to imagine how badly this one could go without more protection from the elements.

Normally, Kurt would just wait until Black Friday (which was only two days away) to go box-hunting, but a gut feeling told him it'd be better not to wait. He stretched his aching limbs and back, preparing to walk the five-mile trek to Easton Heights, where the rich threw out perfectly wonderful boxes and didn't lose sleep over it. Kurt grumbled to himself, walking the cold sidewalk as a biting wind cut his exposed skin.

Unsurprisingly, the 'homeless experience' was not a glamorous one. There were no people to come along and save the day if something went wrong.

No one batted an eye at a vagrant frozen to death at a train station. They just scraped up the cadaver and burned the remains.

Suburban expanses slowly replaced fast-food chain locations and big box stores as Kurt walked through the frigid waste he called life. He had been a moderately successful young man, once. A messy divorce and subsequent heroin addiction did away with *that* effectively. Time was always on his mind, its abstract and cruel nature an ever-expanding enigma lurking in the dark recesses of his mind.

One day, you were kissing the love of your life. Everyone smiled at the sight of you—things were good. But then, the truth turned its ghastly maw, consuming all that you loved in a belch of flame and cinders. Those were the breaks, and the sooner they were accepted, the sooner everyone could go about their lives. As he walked, Kurt felt tears flowing, the wind practically freezing them on his mangy cheeks. "Lord, if I can just find two more boxes, I will be ever-grateful to you," he said with a tremulous voice.

Going with the track record of his life, Kurt was skeptical regarding God intervening. So far, it seemed he only came to gloat and enjoy the suffering of yet another fallen child. Another dreg of humanity drowning in the gutters. *No substantial loss*, many elitists would say while chuckling and drinking bourbon with their golf club buddies.

In the fifty-two years he'd been alive, Kurt had seen *no one* as malicious and cold-hearted to the unfortunate as Nathan Greer. A real estate sales agent turned investor, the only thing that man saw of worth in *anything* was money. A warm place to stay had been less of an issue before he came in, buying out the shelters one by one. Some of those properties were converted into parking garage complexes, but a few hadn't been turned into anything at all.

Kurt mused on this as he made his way to a busy intersection. He pressed the crosswalk button, then tucked his aching hands underneath his arms to warm them. Nathan had bought those properties to keep people like himself *on* the streets. It was a dog-eat-dog world, sure, but with a morally bankrupt man like Greer around, it felt as though the homeless of Boston were target practice. The crosswalk sign lit up, and Kurt crossed as quickly as he could, his ankles cracking painfully.

Arthritis was a real bitch, and so was winter. They were quite the pair—two peas in a pod. An hour of walking had passed, and Easton Heights came into view. It was opulence incarnate—salt to rub in every open wound Kurt had. He scanned the homes, looking for anything that would be of use, be it old newspapers, boxes, or scraps of cloth. Anything would help with the Dread King of the Winter Solstice riding soon.

The houses were all two stories, minimum. Perfectly manicured lawns dusted in snow sprawled as far as the eye could see. Trees were barren of leaves, the scattering blur of autumnal colors diminished by the gray tinge of a cold and cloudy day. Kurt spotted a communal dumpster for the neighborhood in the distance, a wooden fence buffeting the wealthy from the tragedy of looking upon rubbish.

"Bingo. Maybe *this* will be the ticket," he said to himself, blowing his breath out upon his hands as he rubbed them together. His fingers were growing more and more blue with the rapidly descending temperature. He hastened to the 'trash corral', hoping against hope that something good could come out of that so-far wretched day.

Kurt lifted the lid on the dumpster, and tears sprang from his eyes. There were *dozens* of boxes in good shape, all ripe for the taking. Without a second thought, he dove in and began neatly piling what he found outside of the dumpster. With so much, he could help Joe Pascadillo with his shelter, as well. He was so preoccupied with his findings and renewed joy, that Kurt didn't see the man approach from behind. Something hit him in the back of the head excruciatingly hard, and all went black.

Sometime later, rays of fluorescent light crept through the dark shade of Kurt's unconscious state. Pain wracked the back of his skull, and his limbs felt—restricted. Although it pained him greatly, he lifted his head, forcing his eyes open. He instantly wished that he hadn't.

Kurt was one man of ten, all bound to wooden chairs in some subterranean hell. Cheerful white and teal tiles on the wall and floor belied the sinister nature of their holding place. Suspended from the ceiling were slaughter hooks, and grated drains set in the floor every few feet. Dread was ramping up inside of him, and he felt cold and hollow.

A few of the other men were guys Kurt had seen around town, either at a soup kitchen or in line to receive trash bags filled with second-hand clothes. *All of us are homeless*, he thought, connecting the pieces of what little he could see. Wherever they were, it was an enormous structure. Possibly a mansion, given the expensive-appearing solidity of the architecture and sheer size of the basement they were being held in.

"Any of you know where the fuck we are?"

One of the other men asked gruffly. His voice sounded familiar, and when Kurt looked, he saw it was his acquaintance, Joe. Joe's nose had been broken (either through a booze-fueled fight or his abduction, (Kurt wouldn't have been able to guess *which*), his baggy gray sweatsuit covered in blood. Joe's bald head shined under the beams of light, his eyes wild and ready for a fight.

"Joe, it's Kurt. I just woke up. I don't know where we are, but I can tell you it's a big place. Expensive, from the looks of it." Joe looked his way, smiling a bit at the sight of his buddy. "Good to see you, man. Shit circumstances, though." "I'll fucking say. I had just stumbled across a motherlode of boxes when boom—out like a light." He nodded at Kurt's story, saying his was much the same.

As the vagrants all regained consciousness, they relayed the same story. Every one of them had been taken while gathering for the cold wave. No one would say it, but the slaughterhouse hooks overhead cast portents of doom. Someone abruptly halted the low rolling cloud of murmured conversations when a door opened at the top of the stairs.

"Gentlemen! Welcome! This year, *you lot* get to contribute to the giving season!"

He descended the stairs, carrying with him a waft of strong cologne. Kurt's stomach dropped at the sight of him. Nathan Greer walked casually down the stairs, his charcoal gray suit and freshly dressed hair pristine.

Nathan walked into the circle of chairs, standing at its center so all could see and hear him. "I have chosen you men for the highest honor. Do you realize how *lucky* you are?" he said, enthusiastically dripping venom. Kurt watched him, terrified and hanging on to every word.

Everyone was silent, the rich man clearly reveling in the spotlight.

"Well, I'll tell you," he continued, annoyed at the lack of interaction. "I've been making big moves regarding the lower class this year. But for every food bank box that's handed out to struggling, working Americans, there's a homeless person who can't find somewhere warm to rest."

"Yeah, because *you* fuckin' bought out the gahd-damn sheltas!" Joe shouted across the circle.

Nathan whipped his head in Joe's direction, kneeling so their heads were level. "You've just moved to the top of the list, big boy." They glared at one another for a long time, then Joe acquiesced and averted his eyes.

"*That's* more like it," Greer crooned maliciously. "As I was saying—the economy is more in shambles today than it was a year ago, and simply put—the care packages my investing firm gives out each year are beginning to eat into my profits. I can't allow that. So, I'm going to kill two birds with one stone, as they say."

Time stood still, the group of captive men suspended in a Stygian warp of enraptured dread. Nathan's grin was wide, a mockery of all sanity or normalcy. He continued on, heading to a malevolent precipice none of the prisoners could imagine. "I'm going to feed the poor and give the homeless a home—in their bellies. You all shall be stars in the Thanksgiving meals we pass out tomorrow evening."

He laughed, braying like a deranged mule, tears slaloming down his face in a torrent of blackened mirth. All the men bound to chairs snapped from their fearful silence at once, shouting, begging, pleading. The point was moot—a psychopath held their fates in his wretched hands—and no one came to rescue those at the bottom of the barrel.

"Okay, you go first my friend. You're a lucky man!" He mocked, beginning to massage an average-sized cock through his overpriced slacks. Without warning, he pulled out a straight razor, lowering it towards Joe's face. Joe shrieked, writhing in panic. Kurt screamed with him, fearful and helpless in the face of losing another friend.

Nathan sliced his ears off with great ease, tossing the chunks of cartilage to the concrete floor. Once he seemed happy with the volume of his victim's screams, he sliced Joe from ear to ear, severing his carotid artery. Blood geysered in a torrent, the volume and force diminishing in tandem with Joe's pulse. By the time the downpour was but sparse droplets, he was dead, his eyes wide and staring blindly beyond the veil.

"What a fucking rush!" Nathan jeered, his face painted red from arterial spray. He walked over to a control switch, biting his lip as he concentrated. A slaughter hook rolled forward until it was directly above Joe's corpse. It lowered, and when it was halfway down his torso, Greer stopped. He walked over, and cruelly pistoned the razor-sharp hook into the meat between the shoulder blades. The wet, thumping sound was maddening, all silent but for the panic-wrought breathing of the other captive men.

Nathan unceremoniously walked back to the box, pressing another button. Joe's body lifted until his feet hung two feet off the ground.

"Here's something about me you need to know," he said casually as he stripped his dress shirt and coat off. "I don't mind getting my hands dirty to get a job done. In fact—I *insist* on it." He walked to an unseen part of the basement and came back with a rolling cart laden with blades. After a moment, he grabbed a fillet knife that twinkled murderously under the bright lights. He cut rings around Joe's extremities (neck, ankles, wrists), then began pulling the skin and flesh away expertly.

Once nothing but muscle tissue remained, gleaming redly under fluorescent bulbs, Greer slit the belly. Intestines spilled out of the torso, the stench of gastric juices and fecal matter overpowering the remnants of a deep clean using bleach. He slopped all the organs into a pile, then grabbed a circular saw. Joe's corpse first had its pelvis removed, the legs split at hip-center, then the knees. Within ten minutes, Kurt's last friend had been quartered like deer season's first kill.

"FUCK ME, NOW I'M BEAT!"

Nathan said with the Devil's grin. He tossed the blood-splattered tools onto the cart and made his way back up the stairwell. The moment the door closed,

Kurt began working his wrists against the black zip-tie binding them. Something happened—if it was his unanswered prayer now being redeemed, or sheer dumb luck—he didn't care. His restraints weren't fully secured.

Although it still drew blood, Kurt could slip his bound hands. Once they were free, he leaned over his feet and began fighting the zip-tie there. "Whoa, what the fu-" one man softly exclaimed before being silenced with a meaningful glare. In less than five minutes, Kurt was free of his chair. He scampered to the next man, helping him with his bindings. He looked around the room, speaking slowly but clearly.

"When he returns, we have to pretend nothing's different. Once he gets between us all, we sack him. Agreed?"

Everyone nodded assent to the plan. Just as Kurt was sitting back down, the door opened. Sweat poured down his body, adrenaline coursing as the waking nightmare was drawing to an end—one way or another. Nathan was oblivious to the new dynamic of the room he was entering.

"Okay, I've had my medicine! That should keep me from getting so damn winded for the rest of you." He said, wiping residue from his nose.

"So, which one's next? How about you?" Greer grinned, closing on Kurt.

NOW!

Kurt and his vagrants-in-arms moved as one, bringing the rich cunt down hard onto the tiled floor. They were in a tribal berserk state—the reckoning of their sanguine harvest soon at hand. They all grabbed blades, a blur of chopping, stabbing, slicing. In all the excitement, Kurt lost who he was in that all-encompassing moment.

It was Thanksgiving, and the men around the large mahogany table felt true cheer. The soft conversation had gradually accelerated into an excitable roar. Dirty jokes and raucous laughter intermingled with the clinking of glassware. "Dinner is served!" a dark-haired man exclaimed, entering from the kitchen with a dome-covered silver serving tray. The group cheered good-naturedly, many men raising their glasses in a toast.

Kurt leaned over the tray, his hand gripping the handle of the dome. He cast a meaningful look at the surrounding men. "What do you think, boys? Do I get the honors?" They bellowed a resounding yes at him, producing a smile on his silver and stress-lined face. He lifted the lid, steam billowing deliciously into the high-arched ceiling of the dining room.

Nathan's head sat at the center of the entree, and apple clenched in his post-mortem grin. Hunks of slow-roasted leg meat had steamed in heaps, juices still sizzling from their journey through the oven. The men all cooed approvingly, their eyes ravenous and stomachs roaring in unison. "Dig in," Kurt said with a grin.

Nine meat-laden plates were quickly set, and the men ate their feast in silent appreciation. It was much warmer in the main part of the house, and given Nathan Greer's lack of friends or family—it could serve as a home to them all for the foreseeable future. *God's plan comes through when you least expect it,* Kurt thought as he chewed on a tender strand of leg meat.

Kurt and his kinsmen feasted for Thanksgiving. They remembered Joe fondly and let no scrap of the carnage go to waste. As he lifted another delectable morsel on his fork, he pondered. As much as those Twitter-using blue-hairs got on his nerves, "Eat the Rich" had turned out to be an excellent idea

SHOPPING

MADNESS

BY

ANDY H.

*Holy crap...*Mark Wilson thought as he looked outside the window of glass fronting the store.

Out in the frigid rain, a horde awaited. Pushing and shoving each other for a prime position. They were hungry like wild animals.

Three notable fights had broken out already. The police came to disperse the squabbles and take the guilty parties away. Two officers were left as a token gesture to watch over things, but they didn't stay for long. They were trained to handle many situations but this one was beyond them.

It was the one time of year they didn't want to get involved in what was about to happen. One minute they were among the crowd and the next they were gone.

Mark fiddled absently with the door keys as he closed in on the entrance. He took one last look at the faces of his coworkers behind him. Everyone working that night knew in their heart it was going to be a bloodbath. The crowd outside knew the time was drawing near, movements became more rapid, and the people more anxious as the clock ticked closer.

Mark looked out at the dozens of eyes staring back at him. His heart started to race as his breathing became heavy.

THERE WAS NO GOING BACK NOW

He reached for the door handle and placed the key into the lock. The thin piece of metal slid in smoothly and he twisted his wrist to the left.

Nothing.

He tried again without success.

The press of bodies outside was getting more intense, the windows appeared to bow from the pressure. Mark knew it was just a trick of the light. He hoped anyway.

Out of sheer nervousness, he realized he had tried the wrong key. The greedy eyes of the rowdy customers followed his every move. Inserting the correct key he heard the soft click of the mechanism releasing. He pressed the button and watched the large double doors slide apart.

The barrier was breached as bodies spilled into the store, falling and stepping on each other in eagerness to get inside. Mark threw himself to the side as the stampede passed.

People grabbed boxes from shelves, filling their carts as quickly as they could. Metal bounced off metal as

aluminum trollies and baskets barged
past each other.

BLACK FRIDAY was famous for
turning the kindest people into crazed
animals with the intent of getting what
they wanted at any cost.

He looked past the crowds and saw
two men fighting over a large childs doll,
the last from the shelf. Two little old
ladies swinging handbags at people who
got too close to their carts. They stood
back to back looking like a pair of old
wrinkled warriors making a last stand.
Mark shook his head as he gazed around
the store taking in the scenery.

There was shouting, arguing,
disagreements, and above all the beeping
of tills. The cashiers struggled to keep up

with the goods passing over their scanners.

The stockers made their way down the aisles, weaving between shoppers and aiming to refill the shelves. Boxes were wrenched from their hands as they attempted to unload their haul. They had been open for five minutes and were already overrun and struggling to maintain.

Mark moved through the store and headed towards the rear of the building, nodding at Sarah as he passed. She was a pretty thing he had been planning to ask out on a date. She stuck her tongue out and crossed her eyes while pulling an imaginary noose around her neck.

He smiled back and carried on. Mark nearly jumped out of his skin when his best friend George sailed by on a trolley.

"Never going to happen, you're too much of a wuss," George informed him with a smile. His white teeth were slightly stained behind his fleshy lips. His eyes sparkled and his long hair swished over his shoulder as he sailed by.

Shaking his head Mark moved on. Next, he passed Ted Phelps, the manager of the store. He looked haggard, stuck in the middle of an argument between two young mothers who both wanted the same item. Ted had jumped in the middle to mediate.

Not my problem

Mark pushed his way through a staff-only door and watched as one of his co-workers stepped out the back exit with what looked suspiciously like a joint dangling from two fingers.

Mark shook his head and went to the canteen. He pulled out the nearest chair and sat down. He knew he should be on the sales floor with the others, but screw it he thought as he rested his eyes while no one was around.

Marcus propped open the door and lifted the roach to his lips. Cupping his hands he flicked his zippo and lit the end. He took a deep drag and held the smoke in his lungs.

Breathing out he expelled a long stream of smoke into the cold night air.

"Damn, that's good shit."

His voice echoed through the narrow brick alley walls. He had been warned about smoking at work but everyone was too busy to care.

A noise in the dark at the end of the alley made him swing his head in that direction.

"Hello? Is someone there?"

No answer except for his own breathing. He ignored it, but another distant noise caught his attention. He took a few steps from the door.

A figure appeared out of the gloomy darkness. It was a man walking with a quick stride. As the man moved in on Marcus he could see his pinned pupils and beaming whites.

Before he was able to react, two arms shot out and grabbed his face. The stranger opened his mouth and a small black slug-like creature came into sight.

The man's head darted in and lips fastened on his. Marcus felt something slimy and wet wriggle into his mouth and down his throat. His still-lit joint fell from his fingers into a small puddle while Marcus fell to the pavement.

Marcus watched his attacker stand above him, tilting his head side to side until a noise from within the building caught the man's attention. He jerked his head to the open door and proceeded to enter.

Marcus vibrated on the ground, his body convulsing until things began to shut down, his functions slowing and his mind fading to black.

Soon, he was completely still. Then moments later he was on his feet and following his attacker into the store.

Mark's head jerked up from his chest. *Shit!* He thought. He glanced at his watch and saw that he had lost only a matter of ten minutes or so...more of a doze than a proper sleep.

He looked around the canteen with eyes still blurry and stretched to work out the kinks in his muscles. The door was still closed and the sounds had died down from all the chaos.

It was strange that no one had noticed him missing or bothered to come check. Looks like he had gotten away with it.

He stood and cracked the vertebrae in his neck, and walked out the door.

A CUSTOMER STOOD IN THE HALLWAY

"Hello?"

"Hello...can I help you?"

NO ANSWER

It was a woman standing with her back to him. Her hands dangled at her sides with her head cocked at an angle as if she was listening to something.

He took a few steps towards her and froze when her head straightened and she slowly turned around. Her eyes were like chips of blue ice in the light of the small hallway, her face expressionless and vacant. He backed away from her. She mirrored him, closing the distance between them.

He nervously continued towards the door of the break room until he was pinned.

She came closer lifting one hand. Before he could register what she was doing, he pushed her out of the way and barreled through the store's connecting door.

THE AIR ON THE OTHER SIDE OF THE DOOR FELT... *WRONG*

Screams and shouts came from every direction as he honed in on what was happening. His brain tried to dismiss the noise and atrocities of pure terror before him.

Sarah, whom he smiled at just a little while ago, was pinned on the ground by a pair of strangers. One leaned forward and almost tenderly kissed her. She stiffened, her eyes going wide.

George was forced against a series of high shelves by a large balding man with a beard reaching down to his chest. His palms were bleeding as he struggled to keep a large saw at bay from his neck. As the man pushed from the other side the sharp jagged teeth inched closer and closer.

George's eyes widened when he saw Mark. Pleading for help, unlike anything Mark had ever witnessed. The final look in his eyes begging for a savior. Suddenly, another person crashed into them, the blade forcefully dug into his throat cutting off his airway.

The spell of shock temporarily broken forced him to look away. It wasn't as if he was a coward, but time was against him and it happened too fast. He shook his head trying to shake off this surreal haze.

He was dreaming, having a nightmare...he was still asleep. That had to be it. This wasn't happening, it couldn't be happening.

Mark turned and stopped at the sight of the woman that he had shoved earlier. She came through the door while he was stuck in his daze watching the carnage unfold.

Quick as a flash she swung a sharp spear at his face and cut through his shirt digging a furrow into the meat of his upper arm.

He stumbled back and collided with the shelves behind him. He dropped to the floor and looked in time to see the shelf collapsed on top of him. A foreign object smashed hard against his head and everything went black. The shelf acted as a dome, concealing Mark's body inside.

He surfaced slowly, painfully. Moving slightly he could feel the shelves and boxes that covered him lightly shift. Bringing his hand over his face to assess any injuries, a foul odor assailed his senses. A rich coppery smell with something underlying. His palm was wet and red, as if he placed it into fresh paint. He lay in a spreading pool of blood where he had fallen. His brain tried to make sense of the scene.

Thrashing wildly he managed to get himself free from the boxes that were toppled all over him. He crawled out from the protection of the shelf. His feet started to slide from beneath him as he stepped forward onto the remains of people.

Parts that should only be recognized by a surgeon still steamed and smoked in the cool air of the store.

"What the..." He managed to croak out, but that was all he could speak before a figure stepped out from one of the closest aisles.

Mark's eyes widened as his jaw fell open at the sight of a woman covered in blood. Patches of dried carmine clung to her while other spots were still wet.

She turned her head looking directly at him. Her hair was matted to her scalp, and her once fashionable business suit was now torn to shreds. She stumbled forward colliding with shelves like a drunk during happy hour.

In one hand she carried the remains of a severed arm, its stump still bleeding leaving a crooked trail of droplets. The other held something unrecognizable in the bright lights.

As she turned fully towards him, he could make out the three-pronged hand rake from the gardening section. Gripping stubbornly to the sharp tines of the metal were small meaty chunks and strands of hair. The shocking part was that he knew this woman, it was the same woman who attacked him before. Only this time she was looking for him.

Cocking her head to one side she opened her mouth, behind bloody teeth Mark saw several small black leech-like creatures weaving to and fro in the lining of her throat. They attempted to make contact with him before slowly retreating back into the security and warmth of the woman.

She closed her eyes and crouched a little lower. She dropped the severed arm while securing the garden tool with a white knuckle grip.

SHE SCREAMED AND LUNGED TOWARDS HIM

All he could do was watch as the weapon swung down upon him. The moment slowed to a crawl, the blood on the floor saving his life as her bare feet came in contact with the mess causing her to slip. Flying forward unable to control her fall she kept her eyes locked onto his. A crazed light seemed to shine within them.

The rake hit the wooden door inches above his head. The woman continued to topple towards him, her other hand with its long nails reaching for his face.

He rolled to the side just before she landed. With both arms outstretched towards him, she had no way of bracing for the tumble and her head connected sharply where the door met the floor tiles. The impact smashed her nose leaving it in ruins while caving in one cheek. But she wasn't dead.

Her mouth opened releasing several slimy creatures onto the floor. They writhed momentarily, shuddering. Unable to find a host they became still.

He ducked back into some overturned shelves and lay there for a minute...two.

He heard feet stumbling his way.

WAS IT MORE OF *THEM?*

He had no intention of finding out. Covered behind shelves and boxed items, he was sure he couldn't be found. Footsteps became louder before coming to a halt. Peaking around the shelves he could see *them,* searching with flared nostrils sniffing him out like animals. Their gaze swept over him as he stiffened and held his breath.

Their attention turned toward a noise deeper in the store. Shuffling over one another they chased the sound.

Slowly Mark crawled out from his refuge with the rake in sight. He was no hero, no action movie star...hell, he had only been in one fight in his 25 years on

Earth. But, even as these thoughts crossed his mind he found his arm reaching for the tool.

That's when he felt the breath on the back of his neck.
He wanted to run, but knew he wouldn't get far...wanted to fight, but knew there was no chance...wanted to fall to his knees and plead for his life, but knew it would be pointless.

With no options left, he uttered the only word that came to mind. "Please..."

Something hit him on the back of his head and he knew no more.

As he came to, his skull was sore and his mind was a jumbled mess. He cracked open his eyes and looked around. He was in the middle of the store. shelves and items piled around him to form a barrier at least a foot high.

Clothes had been ripped to shreds and strewn everywhere. Consoles, computers, TVs, and once pricey electronics had been destroyed down to their component parts and used as building materials for the small wall.

He angled his head aware he was not alone. He spotted a pair of feet. One bare, the other still sheathed with a sock and shoe...his gaze traveled higher, the movement pushing fresh waves of pain through his skull and neck.

Manager Ted hung pinned to a wooden board attached to the end of a rack of shelves.

Glints of steel glimmered from nails that sat in the flesh of his wrists, elbows, neck, and face. They speared through the fabric of his shirt and pinned his nametag permanently to his left breast.

Mark observed a nail that shot past him and entered one of Ted's closed eyes. He moved his head towards the direction of aim and saw Sarah with a nail gun pulling the trigger sending projectiles into Ted's flesh and bones.

She was like all the others now; tattered and bloody with crazed eyes seeing nothing beyond her own madness.

People rustled around him, some determined and focused on what they were doing, others wandering aimlessly.

A woman pushed a cart ahead of her, stopping and looking at nearby racks. She reached out and plucked a severed head from a shelf and dropped it into her trolley as she walked on.

Mark had a sick feeling in the pit of his stomach when he realized the head belonged to George.

Another man close by noticed he was awake and moved towards him. He bent down and grabbed his neck, yanking him to his feet.

Pulling him close he opened his mouth revealing a nest of leeches in the depths of his throat. He tried to pull back but one of the creatures detached and flew towards his face.
As Mark began to let out a scream,
The creature latched onto his tongue and squirmed its way down his gullet. The man let go and Mark stuck his fingers into his mouth trying to grab it ...he couldn't reach it, it was gone.

HIS FREE WILL WAS STRIPPED IN SECONDS

His hands fell from his face and he looked at the ones around him with a new perspective. He could feel the creature multiplying inside him controlling him.

Walking to the front of the store he stepped through the broken glass of the doors AND ENTERED THE NIGHT.

THE BALLAD OF MAY

HENRY

By

JACOB PITTMAN

It was Thanksgiving Day. Martha Henry came in with mashed potatoes in one hand and cranberry sauce in the other, placing both plates on the dinner table before returning to the kitchen to fetch more. She had a grin on her face that on the surface looked genuine and content, but internally masking something more akin to malice. Sitting across the table was her daughter May Henry, whose blank expression threatened a catatonic state.

"Set the silverware out, darling."

May remained just as still.

"May..." Martha repeated as May flinched back into the nauseous reality of their situation. Martha could see the pain that was festering inside her daughter. Her world collapsing. The horror of the truth ripping her apart, and the terror of what is to come of them should the plan fail.

"Please set the silverware..." Martha said as She fought back tears. All

She wanted to do was grab her and feel the pain together. Let her know She didn't have to hurt this way. But that couldn't happen yet, Martha and May held eye contact for dear life.

That old truck the seasoned man drove came up the driveway. Martha looked out the window and then back to May, wrapping her arms around her.

"You have got to be strong for me. You have to hide this fear deep inside. We cannot screw this up." Then She put both hands on May's face and said,

"IF WE DON'T DO THIS RIGHT AND DO IT NOW, WE ARE AS GOOD AS DEAD"

May pulled herself together.

The door knob jiggled and twisted before coming open. Joe Henry walked in carrying a bag with wine and a loaf of bread sticking out of the top. He had a smile on his face as he came into the dining room. Martha met him and was somehow able to muster a kiss for him. A genuine kiss conveyingeverything was okay. "Hey, hun. Sorry, I'm late. Had to beat an old lady with a stick for this bread." On any other day before this, it would have been funny; now unnerving.

DINNER TIME

All three sat around the dining room table. The turkey had just been pulled out of the oven and was steaming hot in the middle of a nice spread. Turkey dressing and deviled eggs along with sweet potato pie and garlic bread. Martha went all out this Thanksgiving meal. At first, May was thinking it was just part of the plan to get him relaxed buttered up. But as the meal continued, she realized her mother just wanted one last home-cooked meal together.

They ate, laughed, and passed the dishes around. For a little while, things seemed normal. And May smiled for a moment.

"That was amazing. thanks, honey." He said, wiping his mouth. Grease streaked his rosy cheeks as he gazed at his wife with a smile.

Martha looked back, smiled, and then said, "You're welcome...Joe." The tone of her voice behind his first name slayed any hint of normalcy that was left. May's eyes became wide and frightened, and her grip on her own leg was tight, while the grip around the knife in her lap was tighter.

"Hunny, is something wrong?" Joe said.

The stupid look on his face as he spoke with such an innocent tone had made Martha even angrier. She couldn't stand it anymore. She couldn't do it quickly. She had to draw it out until she heard the words from him.

"I hope you enjoyed your meal because it is going to be the last time I ever cook for you." She said with even more intensity.

"Honey, whatever it is, I don't understand," Joe said, confused.

"Stop calling me honey." She stood up and walked around the table to the other end. May remained seated in the center.

"What I'd like for you to do now is shut up, and listen very carefully to what I'm about to say."

Joe put his hands flat on the table. "Okay."

Pouring herself a glass of white wine, Martha took a sip and calmed herself before continuing.

"Where do I begin...For a long time, I couldn't believe it. I didn't want to. I was willing to trust that you were telling the truth when you said you were working overtime...It was around July when you started doing it, wasn't it?"

"Working overtime? Is that what you're mad about?"

"No...I'm talking about what you were really doing Joe."

"Either way, we shouldn't do this in front of May."

"Don't try to sound like a father now. She knows. Do you think that she's stupid too? Just like you think I'm stupid? You walk around thinking everyone is dumber than you, don't you Joe? I bet you felt like you really had the world fooled. You hid a secret that made you feel so superior, didn't you? Can you please cut the shit, shut your lying fucking mouth and let me finish saying what I have to say before it's too late?"

Their eyes locked in battle. She could see the hate inside him twisting alive behind those half-dead eyes. The illusion of love he projected for her vanishing. An illusion that she already saw through.

"At first you came home late. Always with a new excuse. Then, We didn't even talk about it. There was no talking at all. No intimacy. Nothing. I figured you were doing something normal like drinking, gambling, drugs, and maybe an affair. I was in limbo every night." Her eyes began to glisten with tears.

"Finally, I just gave up. You're such a terrible liar you know that? I knew you were up to something...But somehow, you still had me fooled. You fooled all of us into thinking that you were doing normal deadbeat husband and father things...But no. You are far from normal Joe. I don't want to imagine how far you have taken this."

Joe couldn't hide his nerves any longer. Quivering, He reached for the wine bottle, grabbed the glass, and started filling it up with red wine. Martha would continue to lay it on until he broke. She was almost salivating at the thought. Getting everything out in the open. She felt pain, rage, and even a sick pleasure in making him squirm.

"Martha, can we please just,"

"I saw you, Joe...I saw you and that young man go into the shed."

His cup overflowed with red wine staining the white tablecloth with each drop as the fabric soaked it in.

"Martha please..."

"You both went into that shed,"

"Damn it please Martha, not in front of my daughter!"

"...and you were the only one that came out again."

May knew they had just crossed
the point of no return. Her mother was
taking this all the way.

Joe was shaking with sweat
pouring down his face, he was rocking
back and forth in his seat. He took a big
pull of his wine.

"Now you may speak," Martha said
with her chin on her fist, leaning in to
listen.

"Martha...I don't know what you
are talking about. This is a mistake. He
was just someone I met and I was
showing him around the yard. He was a
nice guy..."

"I'm sure he was."

"What is that supposed to mean, huh?"

Martha held her tongue.

"Look...okay, I admit to having an affair. Is that what you want to hear? I admit that I have been distant from you and May...I was stressed out at work. I needed to blow off some steam. But you are suggesting, no, accusing me of something...something that I am not capable of. You have the right to hate me, Martha. I cheated on you. I pushed you away. We can get a divorce if you want. But how can you allow yourself to think I could do something so heinous."

May was shaking.

Martha was gritting her teeth. She had nothing but hatred left for her husband at this point.

"I get up and I go to work all day. I pay the bills and I have to work overtime! I'm stressed out. I have a problem, Martha. It started off with just visits, and then it turned into,"

"Murder..."

He turned completely pale at the word.

"I...I can't believe it,"

"I know it. May knows it. Everyone knows you've been screwing around with young guys. I get calls from my sister checking up on us. I get weird looks from people in public. You never really fooled anyone, Joe. But soon they'll all know what you have been doing to those young men after you are finished with them."

Joe stood up and slammed his fists on the table startling them. .

"Proof...What proof do you have that I could do something like this?"

Martha broke eye contact and looked at May. The horror of it all swelled up in her throat taking her voice away momentarily. She looked into May, who looked back into her mother's eyes seeking refuge. Wishing to just be done with this. Martha found strength in her daughter's eyes as tears bled down her cheeks.

Like a rabid animal backed into a corner, he roared, "What do you think I do Martha? Do you think I lure people here and kill them? Do you think I bury them under our shed? We can go dig it up right now! I've got nothing to hide!"

"I DIDN'T KILL ANYONE!"

"I slept around because I got tired of you, and that is all! I got tired of working 60 hours a week. I got tired of pretending to be someone that I am not...Do you think I don't know what's going on? you're trying to turn our daughter against me!"

"Don't even try that you son of a bitch," Martha roared back.

"You haven't been her father since you raped and murdered a boy her age!"

Joe made a move towards her. She backed around the dining room table, while May shook and gripped the handle of the knife even harder.

"I did not!" Joe said growling through his teeth.

"Then where is he, Joe...If you didn't kill that boy, where is he?..." Martha said with a softer tone.

"If he's still alive, there's still a chance. You can make things right... You can return him to his family. You can turn yourself in and get help."

Tears fell from Martha and May's eyes.

"Tell me I'm wrong...for God's sake tell me that you didn't murder Ethan. Tell me that I am wrong!"

"I don't know what you're talking about." He said with a straight and calm manner that came out of nowhere. Suddenly he appeared to be a different person. It was the *real* Joe Henry. He was present with a cheeky grin across his face.

"And seeing as you have no proof of any of this, I think we're done here. I'm clearly not welcome in my own house that I paid for, so I should just pack my things and go stay with Benny."

He turned around and made his way to the stairs.

"You mentioned the shed," Martha said.

He kept moving up the stairs.

"I never said you buried him here."

He stopped. The grin went away.

"You only killed him there. His body...you haven't figured out what to do with him yet."

Now it was May's move.

He stepped back down the stairs returning to the dining room again.

"Now I really don't know what you're talking about anymore Martha. Either way, whatever it is that you're trying to do, it isn't going to work. So if I were you, I'd let me pack my things and leave."

"You're not going anywhere, Joe."

THAT WAS MAY'S QUEUE

She stood up, clutching the large carving knife.

"What's this?" Joe asked with pressure forming at his chest. His heart began beating slower. May started carving the turkey.

"Joe, I don't need proof. I'm not trying to bring you to justice. I just needed to make you squirm on tape. It would make our story more believable."

May finished cutting the Turkey, and inside was a recording device.

"This part would be cut off the recording at least. But the rest that shows you becoming very defensive and riled up will definitely be enough to go along with our story." Martha stepped around the table to the other side and stood next to May.

"MAY...DO IT!"

She started shaking and then screamed as she plunged the knife into

Martha's abdomen. Joe lunged but fell to a knee. Martha almost screamed in pain herself. "Good girl..."

"NOW AGAIN!"

"Jesus Christ..." Joe uttered as his reality turned to fog.

"How wast he wine...Joe?" Her words softened to a whisper.

He fell to his knees and hands, struggling to fight the poison.

Martha struggled to get her words out and stammered, "I don't even...know if there is a body... Joe...But I proved that you were a monster...confronted by your wife...who you attempted to murder...then May gets a knife...and protects herself..."

Joe drooled as he faded out.

"I got you...to admit...to cheating...the rest...will be confirmed after I survive this attack."

"DIE NOW, I'LL SEE YOU IN HELL ONE DAY"

Joe fell face-first into the hardwood floor, as his heart stopped.

"May...finish it...make it look...like a struggle..."

"May, you have to...do it. He's already dead. Just one good stab in the... throat to make it look real."

She did not move.

"MAY HURRY..."

May stood over her father's remains and looked at him.

"He cheated on you..."

"May...what are you,"

"But you killed Ethan. Remember?"

"We don't...have time for this..."

"We're going to put that body in Dad's shed. We're going to frame him for something you did..."

Martha's wounds had been planned. May was trained to stab her in locations that would cause the least amount of damage to her internal organs.

"You hate him because he cheated on you." May stepped toward her mother who was lying there bleeding on the floor.

"May...what are you doing..."

"You just couldn't stand it, could you? That your husband was cheating on his perfect little wife with a guy."

May clutched the knife with heightened intensity as rage grew within her.

"Your perfect little life was coming to an end. So you'd take everything from him. His house, his money, his daughter, his life, and paint him as a monster."

"May..."

Martha said with fear in her eyes. She crawled along the floor, smearing her own blood leaving a path behind her..

"I know a monster... She murdered a seventeen-year-old to try to make things work. She buried him under the shed. She's been planning this for months. She's the one who manipulated me into helping her."

May stood over her mother. Martha looked up at her daughter and found the face of death staring back at her.

"Our story has changed Mom...Instead of me stabbing him to protect my perfect loving mother who belittles me, who manipulates me, who has made me hate myself, who has murdered my father..."

Martha's eyes widened.

"It ends with you getting what you fucking deserve."

The knife came down again and again. The stabbing didn't stop.

MARTHA HENRY WAS FOUND WITH 264 STAB WOUNDS

May Henry was admitted to the Vinwood Mental Facility after being deemed clinically insane for the killing of her mother and father.

At age 26, She was considered for release after showing improvement and displaying years of good behavior. That was until Nurse Judy Franklin was stabbed to death after what was considered a genuine friendship between the two. The nurse brought Henry a Thanksgiving dinner. This caused her to snap and go into a frenzy. She shattered the plate and used a broken piece to carry out the stabbing.

May Henry is still incarcerated as of this report.

HAPPY THANKSGIVING

ALL SHALT BE

THINE

BY

DAVID E. ANDERSON

Savannah Cross navigated the SUV down a dirt road and pulled up to the farmhouse. She parked alongside a weathered porch and killed the engine. She stepped out into the cool autumn air and smoothed down her denim jacket with a sigh while looking over the barren farmland. This was Savannah's first time laying eyes upon it. From what her grandmother told her, Savannah's family lived on the property for almost two centuries, and her mother, Silence

Cross was born and raised in this house with her brothers and sisters.

It was Thanksgiving day, and Savannah was here to meet the family she knew little about. After exchanging a few letters with her grandmother she cultivated an invitation to meet her late mother's family for the yearly feast.

As the front door flew open crashing into the side of the farmhouse, Savannah caught her first glimpse of an elderly couple she assumed to be her grandparents. Her mother had no photos of them and never bothered to tell Savannah their names.

She knew from the letters that they were Abel and Hepzibah Cross. Abel walked with a cane, his back stooped, but he managed to descend the porch steps quickly. He was bald with a bulbous nose wearing a plain gray shirt and trousers held up by suspenders.

Hepzibah wore a bonnet and an apron over an old blue dress. She was plump with wispy gray hair.

Savannah extended a hand in greeting, but Abel abandoned his cane against the porch and enveloped his granddaughter in a fierce embrace. "I'm so glad you're here," he said with a sob. "Our blessing has returned."

Returned?

Savannah thought, puzzled by the word. She'd never set foot on this property before, so how had she '*returned?*'

Her grandmother wrapped her arms around them both. "Welcome, Savannah. This will be the best Thanksgiving in years, the finest since your mother left us."

"Left you?" Savannah backed out of the embrace.

"I'm sorry, she didn't talk much about what happened. But I was under the impression...well...didn't you force her to leave when you found out she was pregnant at sixteen?"

Grandma Hepzibah's eyes widened in shock. "Oh, no, dear. Nothing could be further from the truth. She was only a child, not much younger than you. We never found out who the father was, but we assumed it was a local from town. Your mother was beautiful and caught the attention of many young men. We were ecstatic when she told us and we welcomed her and her child with open arms. You belong here with us. We're your family."

"So, why did she leave then?"

"Well...I think we can explain," she stammered, looking at her husband. "But...well...let's get started on the feast. You must be starving after that long drive. We'll talk later about this, all right?"

Flanking their granddaughter, they led her inside into a wide dining room where ten others were seated around a carved wooden table. Her grandmother had written that Savannah's aunts, uncles, and their spouses would be joining them for the special day.

They introduced themselves one by one. The only one Savannah had ever heard about was her Aunt Muriel. An older sister her mother had been close to while growing up. Muriel very much resembled Savannah's mother; dark hair, blue eyes, and a thin nose. She was only a couple of years older, but looked older still; with pallid skin and more than a touch of gray in her dark hair. Doing the math, she had to have been in her late forties looking closer to sixty.

It had always been just Savannah and her mother on Thanksgiving. Just the way they liked it and all Savannah ever knew. They always made way too much food and would binge on leftovers for days. The spread of food on the table before her was about the same size, despite being intended for over a dozen. A turkey, some stuffing, mashed potatoes, cranberry sauce, rolls, and a mix of vegetables. No one would leave the table hungry today, but there wouldn't be much in the way of leftovers. For drinks, there were two pitchers of apple cider.

Dishes were being passed around and Savannah took her share. When handed the jug of apple cider she grimaced. The idea of pouring cider into her glass already containing a couple of ice cubes seemed appalling. However, she held her tongue not wanting to appear ungrateful and rude, and poured the cider anyway. When her plate was full, she stabbed her fork into the stuffing but paused when she heard her grandfather clear his throat. She glanced up and saw all were joining hands. She put her fork down, blushing, and joined hands with her grandparents seated on either side of her.

Abel dropped his head and spoke, "On this day of gratitude, we come before you with thankful hearts. Though facing challenges and uncertainties, we trust you will sustain us through these difficult times and look forward to better days ahead. Thank you for returning our Savannah to us, and for restoring our blessing. Amen."

Savannah echoed the amen along with the others and then began digging into the food. The turkey was rather dry, and the stuffing somewhat flavorless, but she thought perhaps it was their way of living "plainly".

In their letters, Grandma Hepzibah spoke of their religious background. They were Quakers, having come from England centuries ago in search of religious freedom. Their family's group eventually broke off from the Quaker church, and they now called themselves "Apostolic Friends". As her grandfather had referenced when saying grace, they'd been going through hard times with bad crops and poor health. He'd said something about their blessing being restored as if suggesting Savannah's return would bring back their crops. She questioned in her young mind if they assumed with the loss of her mother that she'd be moving in with them.

After about ten minutes of eating and small talk, Aunt Muriel asked Savannah if she had any siblings.

"No. My mom never married. She was focused on her career, more than anything."

"Oh, what did she do?"

"She started as a maid at a hotel when I was a baby and ended up running the place a few years later."

"Oh, my, That's impressive!" said Muriel with a smile. "I always knew she was destined for great things."

"She always spoke kindly of you, Aunt Muriel. Do you have any children?"

She looked to her husband, Thomas, then turned back to Savannah with a frown. "We don't, I'm afraid. We very much wanted a houseful of little ones, but we've had...trouble in that area, I guess you could say."

Savannah winced, "Oh, sorry. I didn't mean to get personal."

Muriel gave a forced laugh, then said, "That's okay, darling."

"I noticed there isn't a kids table. I suppose I'm the youngest one here." Savannah was only seventeen, and just recently got her driver's license. Everyone else at the table appeared to be in their thirties at minimum.

They went back to their food, eating in silence. Savannah went back to her own plate, every so often taking a peek and assessing each individual. Any time she made eye contact with the family she felt uncomfortable and awkward.

Grandpa Abel finally broke the silence. "When your mother left, something changed. Our blessing went away."

Blessing

He used that word twice before, in an unusual context both times.

Abel folded his hands in front of him. "We'd always had plentiful crops, strong bodies, and many kids. It had been that way for our family since before my time. But when your mother left...things changed. Our crops withered, and our health worsened. Two of your uncles and one of your aunts have passed on, all dying before they were forty. And children...well, as you rightly pointed out, there's no kid's table."

He suddenly appeared angry, his voice booming "I don't understand why he..." Abel stopped speaking suddenly as if realizing he'd said too much.

"He?" asked Savannah.

Hepzibah gasped, then spoke quickly. "Your grandfather is referring to God, of course."

"Stop!" he said. "We shouldn't lie to her. God has nothing to do with it. God abandoned us, so we abandoned God."

Savannah expected her grandmother, or someone at the table, to object, to call his words blasphemy, but no one spoke up.

Abel continued speaking. "We don't know Savannah well, but she *is* family. And she deserves to know the truth." He turned to the girl, "I'm not talking about God. I'm talking about someone...quite different."

She could see a lot of uncomfortable faces around the table, people glancing at each other as if to say *'Are we really doing this?'*

All was silent for about a minute before Savannah asked,

"Who are you talking about?"

Finally, Abel cleared his throat and recited, *"If thou therefore wilt worship me, all shalt be thine. Luke four-seven."*

Savannah sighed. "I'm sorry if this disappoints you because you seem like nice people, but I'm not really into all that Bible stuff. I guess when mom walked out, she left more than just her family behind."

Abel shook his head. "That wasn't God saying that. Look, we come from a community that was so faithful to God for so many years, doing all He asked, and our reward...well, we were driven out, imprisoned, slaughtered, made to live on scraps, suffered with illness, and lost children. And sometimes it just seemed like maybe there was a better way. God promised great things in Heaven, but life here on Earth was miserable for our people. We'd felt forsaken. This was a century and a half ago after our people had split from the Quakers. Our forefathers, including my grandfather, felt something more had to be done."

"I don't understand," said Savannah. "What did you do?"

"If thou therefore wilt worship me, all shalt be thine. That wasn't God saying it.

Nor was it Jesus. Satan promised great rewards for worshiping him.

"Wait. You're telling me..." Savannah chuckled. "You're a bunch of Satanists?"

There was a hesitation, but eventually, heads nodded around the table.

"Oooookay, so what happened? Obviously, you aren't having any kids, and you said your crops withered and you got sick and people died. So did the devil back out on the deal?"

"It was your mother," said Abel. "When Silence got pregnant and left, that's when the devil forsook us. Abandoned us."

"Why?"

"Because Silence took what the devil wanted."

He looked up at his granddaughter. Savannah glanced around the table and saw all eyes were on her. She knew what they were saying the devil desired.

HER

"The devil always has a price," said Grandma Hepzibah. "It's why we needed you to return. He gives generously to the faithful, but there's always a price."

Savannah dropped her fork to her plate with a clatter, then sat back with a mischievous smirk. "Is this a joke? You people are planning to sacrifice your own *granddaughter* to the devil?"

"We have to sacrifice someone every five years or so," said Abel. "Someone from within our family, not an outsider. Your grandmother and I sacrificed three of our own children. We knew that in order to keep things going, we'd have to sacrifice the firstborn of the next generation. And the first of our offspring to be with a child was your mother. So, you see, it has to be you."

"That's why my mom left," said Savannah. "She knew you were a pack of sick, twisted fucks who think they are in the Devil's league."

"We've seen Satan," Abel explained.

Hepzibah cut in, "How do you feel dear? The dose should be kicking in soon."

Intense eyes waited for a response from Savannah.

"We've drugged you."

Savannah laughed. "Drugged me? When?"

Savannah looked at her half-empty glass of apple cider. She looked around the table and saw everyone else had been drinking cider as well. "I got my cider from the same jug you guys did. "

"Your ice cubes have melted."

Savannah appeared caught off-guard. The room suspected her to fall into a dizzy spell at any moment. She started laughing instead.

"Who the fuck puts ice cubes in apple cider? " She asked while still laughing. Savannah raised her glass to the family to toast them, then she took another sip.

"What's going on?" asked Grandma.

Savannah picked up her cloth napkin and unfolded it to reveal a puddle of water surrounded by a sliver of ice. "I didn't want to be rude." She said with a smirk.

"Well," said Grampa. "A bit outnumbered wouldn't you say?"

"So this is it? This is where you guys attack me all at once, hold me down, and, what, carry me out back and sacrifice me to Satan? Because I'm ready to put up one hell of a fight."
Her grandparents looked around the table, glances thrown in all directions anticipating the next move.

"Would you like to hear the rest of the story? Savannah asked.

"What do you mean?" asked Abel.

"Would you like to know more about my father?" The room began to chill as everyone rustled in their seats.

Savannah shook her head. My father was someone quite important. Someone you all worshiped."

"My father fell in love with my mother and impregnated her. And you were going to kill his daughter. My mother abandoned you, and she wasn't the only one. Daddy took your precious blessing with him, undoing all he'd done for you, and cursing your crops, cursing your bodies, and as you so eloquently put it, drying you up."

"Can you...b..bring him back?" asked Abel stumbling over his words. " "We'll do whatever he wants."

"Oh, I haven't seen my father in years. Satan isn't exactly the most reliable family man. Savannah reached forward, holding her hand towards the Thanksgiving turkey with her fingers splayed. They watched as the bird began to shrivel and collapse upon itself, blackening as if time had sped up the decaying.

Her family gasped and started to rise. Savannah turned her power on them with an invisible force taking away any ability to move.

Abel went first, his eyes sinking back into his sockets as he moaned in agony. His tongue protruded from his mouth, dry as a bone. He choked once, then collapsed forward onto the table, face-first into the cranberry sauce as if seeking any source of moisture.

"Abel!" screamed Hepzibah, reaching for her husband as her fingers began to shrivel. Skin cracking as her body mummified. "Please," she whispered, then fell forward, her fingers snapping off when they hit the table dying next to her husband.

Savannah's eyes turned red as she looked around at her aunts and uncles, all frozen in terror.

"Who's next, bitches?"

In the Name Of

By

Post-Mortem

Saliva splattered its decoration on Elanor's fourteen-year-old face. The man panted like a beast above her as he violently thrust himself inside her virgin vessel. His long, greasy, dark hair flung against the smooth skin of her chest.

She pulled her head away to hide her repulsive disgust. The man drove his head down to her breast. The callused texture of his hand groped and squeezed a handful of her flesh.

Thirty seconds later, he moaned in her ear with a hot breath. Cold chills of fear crawled down her spine. She knew what this meant.

Her father, Malachi, peeled away from the inside of her. He rolled over and stroked his fingers through her hair. He admired her beauty and said, "You have grown to be quite the woman, Elanor. Shall we pray to the God of the fathers that we have conceived?"

She nodded in agreement and listened as he dropped to his knees to recite the prayer. Meanwhile a pool of white cream collected between her legs and slowly dripped out. She fought the urge to vomit, forcing herself to swallow the bile instead.

Almost ten months later, the bloody mucus-covered baby was placed in Elanor's arms. The raw high-pitched scream pierced her ears. She smiles as she looks into the baby's eyes. She created this creature. The midwife instructed her on the care the child would need.

Her father and her sisters watched the birth take place. They clapped their hands together in the celebration. Another member of the family had found its way into the cult of the Smoky Mountains.

Elanor's delight quickly morphed into dread. Her child was the last born of the year. This meant it would be one of the three to be sacrificed in the community Thanksgiving dinner. The child's life was momentary, and this terrified her.

The community family originated from three brothers and their wives. The brothers were filled with hate towards modern society and its culture. They

perceived society had thrown away
morals and religion to fit the model of
the fast-paced and ever-changing
personality of the country.

The brother's religious bigot
mindset had sent them on a mission to
form a strong religion based on sacrifice
and seclusion from the world. Four
generations of inbreeding had led to the
physical disfigurement of some
members.

At the age of their periods, the
female family members were required to
submit to their father's sexual
preferences. By the age of twelve, they
were thrown to the wolves of all the
capable men of the community.
Ritualistic orgies were held until the girl
was impregnated. The last three children
born in the year were sacrificed to the
tree God of the Black Forest.

The cold air blew its breath against the cloaks of the three brothers as they stood in front of the massive weeping willow tree branches. The bright stars glistened in the sky next to the full moon of cascading craters. Their mouths gaped open with amazement as the voices of the spirits within the tree prompted them of the commandments they must follow.

They must make their clothing from the land inside the forest. They must only eat from the fruit and vegetation provided to them. The animals that lived around them would supply the meat. Anything else would be impure and damn their souls to Hell. Only members of the three couples would be pure enough to dwell in the forest's presence. The men bowed in submission to their master and the Smoky Mountain cult was born.

It was the late evening before the Annual Thanksgiving dinner. The dishes were being prepared along with the butchering of the children. The first child was five months old and was a thick chunky baby. The body thudded on top of the chopping board. Small red freckles splattered on the wooden top next to the sweet corn casserole dish.

A woman gathered the sharp meat cleaver from the knife block. Her bony hand wrapped around the handle. She pivoted and turned to the dead child. She made a quizzical face as she attempted to identify the child of the community.

She asked the other woman in the kitchen "Is this Bethany's boy?"

They all answered in broken unison, "Yes it is."

"Oh wow, he's a big kid. They fed him well." The women nodded in agreement.

She raised the meat cleaver above her head. The blade sliced through the air down to the delicate flabby flesh. A Grotesque wet squish followed as the head separated from the neck.

The woman examined the result with nonchalant pleasure. She scooped up the skull and placed it in the ceramic crock pot with the suffocating broth and vegetables. She set the timer to the oven and plugged in the crock pot. She returned to the headless corpse to resume the carving. She found the wire cutters and walked over to the specimen. The tip of the snippers plummeted under the flesh as the wet squishing sound proceeded. She squeezed the two handles together with all her scrawny might. The blades finally cracked the sternum bone when the sweat rolled past her eyebrow. She let out a sigh of relief. She cracked the ribs open and the bloody membrane clung to the walls of the bones. She dug the organs out and put them into their appropriate dishes.

The butcher was able to reach the heart. Just one final pry of the chest cavity, and she would be able to gather the treasured heart. She forced her fingernails under the bloody bone until she had a good grip and pulled apart the carnage.

Body fluids painted speckles of dark red on her devilish face. They all heard the wet seeping sound as she did what was necessary. Her hands held the prized heart in all its glory as the liquid red oozed between the creases of her fingers.

The second sacrifice was cut and carved the same. When it came time for the third child, the old woman became alarmed. The child was missing. She hastily notified Malachi of the circumstances.

It wasn't long before the cult leader tracked down the child. Elanore held her daughter tightly as she breastfed.

The leader asked with his deep authoritative voice, "Elanor, why haven't you surrendered your child to the kitchen?"

She held back the tears and answered the baby's father,

"She's so perfect. I love her, father."

"As you should, it is your child." He could sense her reluctant mind. He walked close enough to lay a strong hand on her shoulder. The vice of fingers clamped around her shoulder bone.

"We must honor Our God," he insisted.

She allowed her eyes to meet the tunnel of purity within the baby's bright blue eyes before she answered.

"May I sacrifice her at the dinner table?"

He thought about the request and spoke, "Yes, bring her to me after the prayer. You must be the one who permits the child's life to the beyond."

She answered, "Yes, Father."

Malachi spoke sternly, "Gather your emotions, girl. We shall honor Our God."

Four long tables at thirty feet in length were surrounded by chairs. The cult community number had grown to the upper seventies. Men, women, and children sat in their chairs as they awaited the commencing prayer to be recited by Malichai.

THE HAUNTING CHANT OF THE BLACK FOREST PRAYER BEGAN

"Oh Father Oh God of the Black Forest. We offer our livestock, and crops unto thee at the feet of thy creation. We sacrifice our three youngest children to the remembrance of Abraham and Issac. We pledge our loyalty to thee no matter the cost. We worship thee with everything we do to reflect the greater good of thy ways. Oh, great father, we bow at thy power."

The table of dishes was full of casseroles, vegetables, and meats resting in the center of the tables. The arms and legs of the cooked children protruded, and the charred fingertips cast shadows above the dish. The feet and toes were buttered with shine over the red-tinted flesh. The extremities appeared to be clawing their way out of the casseroles.

Malachi slid the top off of the crock pot to reveal the sagging baked flesh of the skull. The eyeballs resembled shriveled-up yellow grapes. The cheek tissue fell away and parted ways with the underlying bone as it was slowly cooked to perfection. The leader was pleased with the extravagant cooking and the dish's presentation, his face displayed his satisfaction.

Malachi could see the family members growing with hunger as they licked their lips. He knew they were starving as they had partook in a three-day fasting before the dinner.

The leader spoke,

"We shall eat, once Elanor sacrifices her child."

He motioned for the girl to rise from her seat and deliver the baby to his side. Elanor's pulse quickened as she paused one last time to stare into her child's eyes. The baby smiled and reached for its mother. Elanor's heart beat out of her chest with fear. Her hands trembled beneath the baby. She remained seated.

Malachi commanded louder with all the eyes watching him and waiting,

"ELANOR, BRING THE CHILD HERE!"

His fierce words cut through her ears like razor blades. She knew he was getting irritated with her. It was a matter of time before he snapped with anger. She knew all too well of this anger. She didn't want her death to be added next to her child's. Her feet moved as did her body with the baby wrapped in her arms.

Elanor stopped next to the leader. She again involuntarily hesitated. The crowd observed the reluctant behavior with their astonished faces.

Malachi had enough, he snapped with aggression,

"GIVE ME THY CHILD!"

he was about to pry the baby from her arms when she surrendered the baby to him. He was finally relieved of his irritation. The baby began crying for its mother.

Malachi sat with his husky figure in his chair. He raised the child above his head and demanded,

"GATHER THE BLADE, ELANOR."

She did as she was told. She picked up the sharp glistening blade and looked at it. The crowd watched in anticipation. The veins in her neck pulsated under the skin as her nerves reached their maximum volume. Her hand was dripping sweat as she held on tightly to the knife.

She stared at the smiling face of her father as he held the crying baby against the table. She thought how could this man be smiling when his daughter was about to be slaughtered in front of him?

An idea raped her mind. She looked at her crying baby once again as she drew back the blade. Her hand sent the knife down. The sharp edge sliced through the skin, forcing blood to gush and splatter across the dishes and the faces of those who sat nearby.

She savagely slashed and slashed away at the flesh. Chunks of gore tore and flew across the table. Malachi's hands dropped with dead weight to his side, a fountain of blood showered the clothes of the leader.

The Crimson liquid ran down Elanore's face, a sign of victory.

The blade made a wet clink sound as it dropped to the ground. She picked up her crying baby with motherly comfort.

The cult elders quickly rose to their feet and darted for her.

She belted out a command as the awe-struck crowd stared at the mesmerizing sight of Malachi dead in his chair.

She demanded loudly, "No! The tree of the Black Forest commanded me to kill him. It was the ultimate sacrifice for our Thanksgiving dinner. God told me that there would be a famine of meat in the next few months because we have killed off all of the animals around us.

Father Malichi will feed us until the livestock is replenished. Rejoice, My Baby will be your new Queen!"

The elders halted to an abrupt stop. They observed each other and concluded the events were valid. The men dragged the dead body of Malachi to the smokehouse.

THE END

Printed in Great Britain
by Amazon